Danny and the Kings

Susan Cooper
illustrated by Jos. A. Smith

MARGARET K. McELDERRY BOOKS
New York

Maxwell Macmillan Canada
Toronto

Maxwell Macmillan International
New York   Oxford   Singapore   Sydney

ALSO BY SUSAN COOPER AND JOS. A. SMITH

Matthew's Dragon

OTHER PICTURE BOOKS BY SUSAN COOPER

The Selkie Girl
The Silver Cow: A Welsh Tale
Tam Lin

All illustrated by Warwick Hutton

NOVELS BY SUSAN COOPER
The Boggart
The Dark Is Rising
Greenwitch
The Grey King
Seaward
Silver on the Tree
Over Sea, Under Stone
(paperback edition only)

(MARGARET K. McELDERRY BOOKS)

Text copyright © 1993 by Susan Cooper   Illustrations copyright © 1993 by Jos. A. Smith

Margaret K. McElderry Books
Macmillan Publishing Company
866 Third Avenue
New York, NY 10022

Maxwell Macmillan Canada, Inc.
1200 Eglinton Avenue East
Suite 200
Don Mills, Ontario M3C 3N1

Macmillan Publishing Company is part of the Maxwell Communication Group of Companies.

First edition   Printed in Hong Kong by South China Printing Company (1988) Ltd.   10 9 8 7 6 5 4 3 2 1   The text of this book is set in Berkeley O.S. Book.
The illustrations are rendered in watercolors. Library of Congress Cataloging-in-Publication Data
Cooper, Susan.   Danny and the Kings / Susan Cooper ; illustrated by Jos. A. Smith.
  — 1st ed.
    p.   cm.
  Summary: While trying to get a Christmas tree for his little brother, Danny receives unexpected help from three friendly truck drivers.
  ISBN 0-689-50577-9
  [1. Christmas trees—Fiction. 2. Christmas—Fiction. 3. Brothers—Fiction.]   I. Smith, Joseph A. (Joseph Anthony), date, ill. II. Title.
  PZ7.C7878Dan 1993   [E]—dc20   92-22744

Danny lived in a trailer near the highway, with his mother and his little brother Joe. Every morning, on her way to work, Danny's mother took Joe to spend the day with Luanne, who lived next door and didn't go to work till the evening. Then she drove Danny to school.

Danny liked school. Christmas was only a few days off, and in the school lobby there was a big Christmas tree with lights shining in its branches. Danny wanted his mother to buy a little tree like that for the trailer, for Joe to see, but his mother said she couldn't afford it. "I bought presents for you both, honey," she said, "but there's no money left for a tree."

At school, Danny's class was rehearsing a play about the first Christmas, when the baby Jesus was born in a stable. In the play, Danny was one of the Three Kings who brought presents of gold and spices to the baby. His friend Steve played a shepherd who brought the baby a lamb. Joe had lent them the lamb.

Steve was a quarrelsome boy. At rehearsal, he told Danny that the shepherds were more important than the Kings, because babies like lambs better than gold and spices. Danny said that wasn't true, so Steve punched him, and made his nose bleed. Their teacher was cross. She said shepherds didn't punch their friends, especially at Christmas, and that of course the Three Kings were important. She said, "My old grannie even used to say that those Three Kings are still traveling the world, carrying presents."

"Is that true?" Danny said.

"I doubt it," said his teacher.

Danny said, "If they are, I wish they'd bring my little brother a Christmas tree. My mom says we can't buy one this year."

Steve was feeling bad because he'd punched Danny. He said, "I can get you a Christmas tree!"

"You *can*?" Danny said.

When school was over, Danny was supposed to walk home, but instead Steve took him on the school bus to his own house, and they dug up a little tree from the garden. Steve said his father wouldn't mind, because there were so many. He found a pair of wheels from an old skateboard and they tied them to the tree, so Danny could pull it home.

Danny was delighted. Off he went, tugging the tree behind him. But the school bus had crossed the highway to reach Steve's house, and Danny's house was on the other side. He couldn't find a place to cross back again. The sky was growing dark now, and snow was beginning to fall. A huge truck almost ran Danny down on its way into a truck stop, and as he jumped aside he had to let go of the little Christmas tree. It fell under the truck's wheels and was smashed to bits.

The truck driver was frightened that he might have hit Danny, so he yelled at him. Danny was frightened, too, so he cried. This made the truck driver feel sorry, so he stopped yelling and took Danny into the truck-stop café. Just inside the door a waitress passed them on her way to the kitchen. She paused. "Hi, Jake!" she said to the driver. "How're the kids?"

Then she looked at Danny, and her eyes widened. "Danny!" she said. "What are you doing here? What's wrong?"

Sniffing, Danny looked up. It was his next-door neighbor, Luanne.

"Hi, Lu," said Jake. "He's okay, he just had a shock. Why don't you bring Danny here some hot chocolate—and coffee for me."

"Sure thing," said Luanne.

Jake took Danny to sit at a table with two other truck drivers. "This is Bud and that's Richard," he said. "We're driving east together."

Danny sniffed. "You squished my tree," he said to Jake.

"You're lucky I didn't squish *you*," Jake said. "What tree?"

So Danny told them how he had wanted a Christmas tree for his brother Joe, who was too little ever to have seen one before.

The three big men listened to him seriously.

"That's a nice thing to want to do," Richard said.

"Sure is," said Bud.

"Yep," Jake said. They all looked at one another, and nodded their heads.

Luanne came with the coffee and hot chocolate. "Shouldn't you be home, Danny?" she said. "Your mom picked up Joe an hour ago. She said she was taking you to your school play tonight."

"The play!" Danny said in horror, jumping up. "I forgot! I have to go!"

"We'll take him home, Lu," Jake said. "Time we got going anyway."

"The trailer camp, down the road on the right," Luanne said.

Danny and the three drivers went outside. It was still snowing. Jake picked up Danny like a parcel and put him in the cab of his big truck. It had a string of colored Christmas lights around the windshield, and above the lights a big printed name: KING OF THE ROAD. Danny felt very important up there, as if he were sitting on a throne. They drove to the trailer camp, and behind them came Bud's truck and then Richard's, each with a string of colored lights around the windshield and the same name: KING OF THE ROAD.

Danny's mother was cross with him, because she had been worried. But Jake explained, and then he gave them all a ride to Danny's school. Bud and Richard drove their trucks in line behind them. Little Joe was very proud to be riding up in the cab of the huge truck. He looked out at the dark sky, at a light twinkling through a break in the clouds.

"Look at the big star!" he said.

"That's not a star, it's a planet!" said Danny. "We did it in school. It's Venus."

"It's a star!" said little Joe.

Jake dropped them at Danny's school. "Okay, Danny," he said. "You be a good King, now."

"Come watch our play," said Danny.

Jake smiled, and shook his head. "Got to go," he said. "We're traveling east."

And the three big trucks drove off in a row, down the road, toward the star that shone brighter than all the rest in the dark sky.

Danny and his class acted their Christmas play for the audience of parents and families, and it was a big success. When everyone was clapping at the end, little Joe escaped from his mother's lap and ran down to the stage to smile up at his big brother. "Hi, Danny!" he said.

"Sit down, Joe!" Danny hissed at him. "I'm not Danny, I'm one of the Three Kings!"

"Hi, Danny!" said little Joe, beaming.

When they came out of the school, the snow was thick on the ground, but the sky had cleared. All the world was white, under the moon and the bright eastern star. Danny's teacher drove them home, and dropped them at the entrance to the trailer camp. "Merry Christmas!" she called as she drove away.

"Merry Christmas!" Danny called. Then he burst into tears.

"Oh Danny, honey!" said his mother. She put down little Joe, and he toddled off toward their trailer. She put her arms around Danny. "Don't cry," she said. "You were so good in your play."

"I had a Christmas tree for little Joe, and I lost it!" Danny wailed. He told her the story of the tree Steve had given him, and how it had fallen under Jake's truck.

His mother hugged him. "Little Joe may not have a Christmas tree this year," she said. "But he's got the best big brother in the world. Your daddy would have been proud of you."

Suddenly they heard a small, excited voice from the trailer, calling to them. Little Joe was standing at the top of the steps, in the doorway, staring in through the open door.

"Mommy!" he called. "Come see! Come see!"

Danny and his mother trudged across the snow. They looked up, past little Joe. And inside the trailer, glowing like a welcome, they saw a beautiful little tree, with a star on its topmost branch.

Little Joe laughed in delight. "Danny! We got a Christmas tree!"

Danny gazed up at the tree, astonished. It was wonderful, far prettier than the tree he had lost. Where had it come from?

He looked about him, at the white snow lying in drifts around the trailer. It was smooth and deep, and there were no tracks in it except the line of footprints from Joe's small feet. But lying on the very top of the snowbank next to the trailer, like a bright jewel in the whiteness, he saw a small, red light-bulb, just like those which had glittered around the windshields of the three big trucks.

Danny smiled. He said softly, into the night, "Thank you, Three Kings."